HOME FARM PUPPIES
Toby Takes The Plunge

Home Farm Twins

Home Farm Puppies

Toby Takes The Plunge

Jenny Oldfield

Illustrated by Kate Aldous

**Hodder
Children's
Books**

a division of Hodder Headline Limited

A Catalogue record for this book is available from the British Library

ISBN 0 340 79601 4

Typeset by Avon Dataset Ltd, Bidford-on-Avon, Warks

Printed and bound in Great Britain by
The Guernsey Press Co. Ltd, Channel Isles

Hodder Children's Books
a division of Hodder Headline Limited
338 Euston Road
London NW1 3BH

One

'Sweet!' Hannah sighed.

'So cute!' Helen breathed.

'Don't get carried away,' their dad warned. 'Remember, this visit is on a strictly look-but-don't-touch basis!'

The twins ignored him and carried on gazing and goo-gooing at three sleeping pups. The one on the left was creamy brown, the one in the middle was a mixture of black and brown, and the third pup was white and black with speckly grey spots on his front legs.

'Look, this one's exactly like Speckle!' Hannah murmured.

Helen felt her heart melt at the sight of the third puppy. 'Mini-Speckle!' she echoed. 'Is that cool, or what?'

Hannah's brown eyes sparkled as she turned to Mandy Steele, the proud farmer's wife who owned the puppies. 'What's the speckly one's name?'

'Toby. And the cream one is Tess. The little brown-and-black one is Titch.'

From amidst the warmth of their soft red blanket, Titch stirred. He opened one eye and cocked one brown ear. Then he opened his pink mouth and yawned. To his right, Toby whimpered in his sleep. The sound drew their mother from the far side of the Steeles' kitchen.

Mandy made way for the anxious crossbreed who padded across the stone-flagged floor. One look told Helen and Hannah that it was the tousled, cream-coloured pup who took after her mother – Tess had the same shaggy, pale-fawn coat and soft, whiskery face.

'And this is Leila.' Mandy rounded off the introductions. She gave the dog a gentle pat as she nosed her way into the middle of the small knot of people and snuffled up to each of the pups in turn.

'We rescued Leila from a plastic cement sack. It had been tied up with rope, then thrown into a river,' Mandy explained. 'The previous owner had obviously wanted rid of her and thought this was the quickest way to do it.'

'That's cruel!' Helen was shocked. 'How could anyone do that to such a gorgeous dog?'

'Or to any living creature!' Hannah added.

Their dad frowned and tutted, but said that it didn't surprise him. 'In my opinion, people should pass a strict test before they're allowed to own pets,' he muttered. 'It would save a lot of suffering.'

'Did you fish Leila out of the river all by yourself?' Hannah asked Mandy, who was small and pretty, with light-brown, almost blonde hair and big grey eyes.

Mandy shook her head. 'No, Jack was the hero. He saw something struggling inside the sack, so he scrambled down the riverbank, held on to a low branch and eased himself out over the water. He grabbed one end of the rope just in time. A couple of seconds later and the whole thing would have been swept away on the current.'

'Wow!' Helen felt herself heave a sigh of relief.

'Look at Leila now – happy, healthy and being the perfect mother.'

As if she knew they were talking about her, the gentle dog stopped fussing over her babies and came up to ask Helen for a stroke. Helen felt Leila's wet black nose push against her palm, smiled and quickly obliged. 'Who's a clever girl?' she whispered.

'Can I pick Toby up?' Hannah snuck in a quick question.

'Hannah!' David Moore warned again. 'I know you. Once you start cuddling one of those pups, you'll never want to put it down.'

'I will, honest!' she protested. Her fingers itched to stroke the tiny warm bundle of fur.

'Your dad's probably right.' Mandy stepped in. 'The puppies are all asleep again. It's best not to disturb them.'

'OK, so can I open the door and let Speckle come in?' Helen changed tack. She knew they'd have to wait until another day before they were allowed to do the cuddles.

Mandy Steele smiled kindly. 'Yes. I reckon the puppies' father has a right to see them.'

If there'd ever been any doubt about who was the

father of the Keld House litter, that had all vanished now. As Helen had said, Toby was a mini-version of his dad, right down to the last speckle on his front paws.

So she sped across the kitchen to the outside door, opening it a crack and feeling the blast of ice-cold air enter the room as Speckle slipped inside. Then, as she tried to close the door, she felt the force of someone else pushing from the other side. Standing back, she let Mandy's husband, Jack, enter.

'Brr, it's freezing!' Jack shivered as he took off his heavy woollen jacket. The new owner of Keld House was short and stocky with cropped, dark-brown hair. 'I suppose I should say Happy New Year to you all, and I will, once I've thawed out a bit!'

'Happy New Year, Jack!' David Moore told him with a friendly grin. 'And I wish you luck with this place!'

'I'm going to need it,' Jack grunted, glancing round at the paint peeling from the walls. 'The last owners didn't go in much for decorating and home improvements!'

The Steeles had only lived at Keld House since

the autumn. Their move from nearby Silcott village had taken place soon after Mandy and Jack had married. Jack was a farmer's son himself, and reckoned he could make a go of hillfarming on the side of Skrike Fell. It would be a tough, lonely life, but both he and Mandy had decided it was what they wanted to do.

'You're right there,' David admitted, taking in the exposed wiring and wonky plumbing in the old-fashioned kitchen. 'If you need a hand with anything—'

'—*Don't* call Dad!' Helen and Hannah chimed in. They giggled, then went red.

'Thanks very much!' he grumbled. 'My DIY skills aren't that bad, I'll have you know.'

'Yes, they are!' Helen told Jack Steele.

'Bedroom shelves, oven door, rabbit hutches . . .' Hannah began a list of their dad's home improvement disasters since they'd moved in to Home Farm.

Jack laughed. 'Anyhow, I won't be doing much until the weather improves and I've got the spring lambing out of the way.'

'Girls, look at Speckle!' Mandy drew their

attention back towards the basket where the three puppies slept.

They gathered round to watch their own beloved Border collie quietly approach the litter. Leila had taken up position beside the basket and kept a wary eye on the newcomer.

Hannah edged forward to ease Speckle's first introduction to his two sons and daughter. 'Aren't they gorgeous?' she cooed, going down on to her knees and resting an arm round his neck.

Speckle stared at the puppies and gently wagged his tail. He put his head first to one side then the other to get the best view of each in turn.

'Meet Titch, Tess and Toby,' Helen whispered. 'They're four weeks old.'

Speckle inched forward, keeping a wary eye on Leila.

The mother gave a low growl, but kept her distance.

'*Snuffle-snuffle*' – Speckle sniffed the rim of the basket, then poked his black nose against the red blanket.

Toby, the nearest pup, stirred. He opened his eyes and stared straight at Speckle.

Speckle leaned in closer still.

Snap! Leila darted forward to protect her pups. Speckle ducked out of the way of her pointed white teeth.

'Close!' Hannah gasped as Leila stood guard.

Her dad smiled. 'Like I said, it's a question of look but don't touch, at least until Momma Leila says it's OK!'

'How long?' Hannah asked.

'Another six weeks at least,' Mary Moore answered, above the loud hum of her sewing-machine.

'Six weeks before we can visit the pups again?' Helen wailed. ' 'S not fair! Speckle is their dad, after all.'

Their mum concentrated on the new tablecloths she was making for The Curlew. The café was closed until February, which gave Mary a few weeks to freshen things up besides taking a well-earned rest. 'Fair or not,' she replied, 'Jack and Mandy Steele are busy people. They don't want you two showing up and pestering them every other day.'

'Bu-ut!' Helen objected. It was five whole days

9

since their visit to the Steeles' remote farmhouse, and like Hannah, she was longing to see Toby, Tess and Titch once more.

'Your mum's right,' their dad insisted. He was sorting through the bundles of photographs which he'd just printed, looking for a good close-up shot of hedgehogs building their nests out of twigs and leaves. He would send off the best pictures to the editor of a wildlife magazine. 'In any case, I was talking to Luke in the village shop earlier, and he told me that Keld House and all the other farms on Skrike Fell are completely cut off by snow.'

'Poor things,' Mary added with a shiver. Then she pressed the pedal of her machine and ran up another long, straight seam.

'Hey Dad, did you print the photos of the puppies?' Hannah seized one of the bundles. Before they'd left Keld House a week earlier, he'd brought out his camera and taken some pictures of proud Speckle with his offspring.

'Here.' David had already separated them from the pile. He handed the photos to Hannah who spread them out on the rug beside the stove.

'There's Titch!' Helen looked over her shoulder

and jabbed her finger at the nearest picture. The little black-and-brown pup stared out from the photo with the biggest, brownest, sweetest eyes.

'Come here, Speckle!' Hannah invited him to join them. 'Do you know who this is? This is your son Titch, and that's Toby, and here's Tess.'

Speckled wagged the white tip of his tail, while the twins' mum and dad looked up from their work and gave a hopeless sigh.

'Jack and Mandy are taking good care of the puppies!' David Moore insisted for what he reckoned must be the twentieth time in two weeks.

The snow was melting from the fells at last, and the twins were driving back from Nesfield with their dad one Saturday in late January, when they spotted Jack Steele driving his Land Rover through Silcott.

Hannah and Helen had waved and yelled hello, but a busy-looking Jack had driven on without stopping to talk.

'Couldn't we just go and see?' Helen pleaded. 'Toby and the others are nearly seven weeks old. They must be ginormous by this time!'

'Maybe in another week or so,' their dad

conceded, turning left at the junction for Doveton. 'Wait until they're two months old – that's next weekend. Then maybe we'll drop in at Keld House with copies of the photographs. Mandy would probably like to see them.'

'Another whole week!' Hannah groaned. She'd pinned pictures of Toby, Tess and Titch on the notice-board above her bed. Now she lay on her stomach, gazing up at them.

Helen had already drawn a row of seven squares on a sheet of yellow paper and marked the boxes with a day of the week. As each day passed, she would put a giant cross in one of the squares. 'Watch out, Socks!' she warned, as their little tortoiseshell cat padded softly across her chart.

'And that's if – IF – the snow melts and there's no frost *and* Dad doesn't have anything better to do next Saturday!' Hannah moaned. All through January her head had been filled with visions of Speckle's three sweet puppies – of Titch playing hide-and-seek under her bed, of Tess snuggling upon her pillow and Toby snoring on the rug by the kitchen stove.

'Dream on!' Helen said when Hannah rolled over

on to her back and confessed her secret desires. 'You know what Mum and Dad are like about having more pets. It's like: "Never again"!'

Hannah nodded and stared at the ceiling. 'Yeah, but they always say that,' she murmured, refusing to let go of her dreams. Toby scampering after Speckle amongst the spring flowers in Home Farm Meadow. Titch learning to sit up and beg for a doggy treat. Tess barking at the red postman's van when it drove into the yard . . .

'You know what they're like,' she insisted. 'Especially Dad. Between us, we can usually get him to change his mind . . .

Two

'No!' David Moore said. 'And when I say no, I mean no!'

Helen sat hunched in the back of their rattling old car as it drove the final half-mile up the icy track to Keld House.

The big, square farmhouse sat on an exposed ridge, overlooking Doveton on one side and the village of Silcott on the other. Saturday had come and the visit been arranged by phone. Helen and Hannah were to see Speckle's three gorgeous pups once more.

'I told you not to mention it before we arrived!' Hannah hissed. 'I said he was in a bad mood because of that flat tyre we had outside Luke's shop.'

But Helen had come out with the question that had been playing on her lips ever since they'd set off from Home Farm – 'Dad, if the puppies are ready to leave their mother, please, *please* can we adopt one and take him home?'

No. Out of the question. 'End of story. OK?' David sat sternly behind the wheel while the car bumped and shook over the rocky road.

'Plee-eease!' Helen whined. She realised Hannah was right; it had been too early to ask. Better to have waited until his heart had been softened by the sight of the three furry angels nestled in their basket. But the question had popped out without her really meaning to let it.

'N–O, no!' he repeated. 'Don't you think we have enough on our hands already?'

Helen sniffed, as if choking back tears. 'You're saying you don't like Speckle, Socks, Solo, the geese, the hens, the rabbits . . .'

David pulled up in the frosty yard of Keld House. A water trough in one corner was still frozen solid and puddles were smooth sheets of ice. 'I didn't say I didn't like our pets,' he insisted.

'Yes, you did!' Helen whinged.

'No. I simply meant that they take a lot of looking after. And they're expensive to feed.' Her dad skidded on a patch of ice as he went to knock on the Steeles' door.

'Back off!' Hannah warned Helen in a low voice. 'Before you put him in a really, really bad mood!'

In any case, they'd spotted Jack Steele emerging from the barn, his sleeves rolled up in spite of the freezing temperature. The friendly young farmer greeted them warmly and invited them to take a look in the barn before they went into the house.

'Mandy's gone shopping in Nesfield,' he explained. 'She should be back soon. Meanwhile, what do you think of these little beauties?'

Following him into the big stone building through double doors, Hannah and Helen could hear the flat, dull bleat of sheep. Higher and fainter, they could also pick out the tiny call of newborn lambs.

'These are the first of the year,' Jack told them proudly, approaching a row of wooden stalls lined with clean, yellow straw. Inside each one was a weary looking ewe and a young lamb. The babies were still wobbly on their legs, their cute faces black as soot, their tiny bodies white and fluffy.

'Do you have to keep them inside because of the weather?' Hannah asked.

'Yes. The newborns couldn't stand the snow,' the farmer told her. 'These older Herdwick sheep can hunker down in a drift or in the lee of a wall. They survive quite well, so long as they're out of the wind and I take them plenty of feed.'

'So you drive the tractor out on to the fell in all weathers?' David obviously admired the hardiness of both sheep and farmer. 'Besides being on hand twenty-four hours a day to help with the lambing.'

'Mandy does most of the lambing work.' Leaning on the waist-high side of the nearest stall, Jack watched happily as a lamb sought out its mother's teat and began to suck greedily. 'To see her you'd think Mandy'd been farming sheep all her life, instead of this being her first year.'

Though she loved the newborn lambs, Helen was eager to get inside the house. 'Erm, can we go now?' she pestered.

Hannah jabbed her with her elbow to make her

wait. After all, Helen's impatience had already almost
blown it for them. It would be a tough job now for
her to work on their dad's soft side and get him to
say 'yes' to taking a puppy home.

So Helen bit her tongue and all three traipsed after
Jack across the yard to the house. They paused in
the doorway to kick off their boots, then tiptoed
into the kitchen.

The first thing they saw was Leila snoozing in an
alcove beside the fire. The creamy mongrel lay with
her whiskery chin resting on her front paws, one
ear cocked, the other flopped forward over one eye.

She heaved a sigh but didn't move as Helen and Hannah crept forward.

'She's worn out, poor thing,' Jack remarked. 'Looking after these three pups has really taken it out of her.

'But where are they?' Hannah asked. She'd just spied the puppies' empty basket.

'Probably up to mischief somewhere.' As Jack put on the kettle to make a pot of tea, a sudden storm of high-pitched yapping came from under the table. 'There's your answer!' he grinned.

So Hannah and Helen went down on all fours to peer into the shadows.

'*Yip-yip-yip-yip!*' Tess sat on the red blanket that the pups had dragged from their basket. She barked crazily while Toby and Titch seized a corner with their teeth and tugged hard. Together they dragged Tess and the blanket along the smooth stone flags.

'*Grrr-rrrr!*' Tess resisted.

Titch and Toby pulled with all their might.

Bump! Tess collided with the table leg, yelped and jumped clear of the blanket.

'Ouch!' Helen winced.

Shaking herself all over, Tess took a few wobbly

steps across the room, while Titch and Toby rolled and tangled themselves in the folds of the torn and tattered bedding.

'Aaah!' Hannah laughed at the puppies' antics.

'Do they always have this much energy?' David asked the farmer with an exhausted sigh.

Jack nodded. 'Now you understand why Leila is so tired. On top of which, she's still feeding them. As a matter of fact. I'm a bit worried about that. Her milk seems to be drying up and the pups may not have been getting enough to eat these last few days.'

His train of thought was broken by the arrival of Mandy Steele. The twins saw her through the window, propping her bike against the wall and lifting a bag of shopping out of the basket attached to the handlebars.

'Quick, grab the pups!' Jack ordered. 'Don't let them get out when Mandy opens the door.'

While Hannah dived for Titch and Helen took hold of Tess, their dad tried a diving tackle on little Toby and missed.

'Hold it!' Jack warned his wife. Then, when he saw David finally pounce on the speckled pup, he yelled that the coast was clear.

Mandy came in with her heavy bag. She smiled as she saw their visitors hanging on to the squirming pups. 'They've livened up a bit since you last saw them,' she commented. 'Gone are the days when they just slept and fed, worse luck!'

Secretly Hannah and Helen didn't agree. If before they'd already decided that Speckle's three pups were sweet and cuddly, they now thought the puppies were totally adorable – the most lovable, wriggly, tumbling, scrambling, tussling creatures they'd ever seen.

Hannah hugged Titch and stroked his warm, silky fur, felt his tiny tongue lick her hand. Helen held Tess close to her cheek and made clicking sounds with her tongue. The creamy puppy squirmed with delight.

'Whoops!' their dad exclaimed as Toby the acrobat nimbly escaped from his grasp.

'He's the adventurous one,' Mandy told them. She'd put down her shopping and taken off her grey-and-red fleece hat. 'He's already managed to climb up into the sink and almost drown himself in a bowl of soapy water!'

Toby raced across the floor and clambered over

his sleepy mother. He settled into a warm space at her side as if butter wouldn't melt in his small pink mouth.

'Tea!' Jack announced, putting the freshly made pot on the table.

'And chocolate cake!' Mandy produced a box tied with pretty ribbon. 'I bought it from your mum's café,' she told the twins, 'so we know it's going to be really fresh and tasty. How about a nice big chunk?'

'Why didn't you ask?' Helen whispered crossly.

The visit was over, their dad standing on the Steeles' doorstep saying goodbye.

Hannah climbed into the back of their car. 'Because!' she retorted, then sealed her lips shut.

'Because what?'

'Because you'd already ruined it by asking too soon.'

'Didn't!'

'Did!' The truth was, Hannah just hadn't found the right time.

All through the tea and cake, the puppies' tricks had kept them on their toes. Titch had tangled himself in the lacy hem of the tablecloth and almost pulled the whole thing down. Toby had climbed on to the work surface, crept along to the sink and was about to perform his diving-into-the-bowl trick again when Hannah had leaped up and stopped him. As for Tess, she'd attached herself to the toe of Helen's grey woollen sock and chewed it happily.

'You didn't even try to find out if we could have one of them at Home Farm!' Helen scowled. She fell silent as she saw their dad come towards the car.

'OK, if it'll make you happy I'll ask him now, Hannah decided, crossing her fingers and hoping with all her heart.

She watched him get into the car, search for his key, put it in the ignition. 'Da-ad!' she began as the engine coughed and choked.

He tried again with the cold engine. 'Hmm? Did somebody speak?'

More spluttering and wheezing. Then the engine began to turn.

'I did,' Hannah said. 'Dad, we were wondering – that is, Helen and me were just talking – I mean, those puppies are so gorgeous – erm, couldn't we maybe, just possibly – is there the teeniest-weeniest chance . . . ?'

'N-O, no!' her dad said. 'And don't go asking your mum. She agrees with me on this. We don't have room for another single animal at Home Farm. Do I make myself clear?'

Three

Hannah and Helen's dad was right about one thing – the animals they had at Home Farm took a lot of looking after.

That winter, though the twins kept them safe and warm in the barn, both Solo their pony and Stevie their donkey got mud fever. It was an infection of the skin round the top rim of their hooves – an itchy red patch which needed daily lashings of antiseptic cream to cure it.

Then there was an hour of mucking out to do every morning before school. Helen and Hannah took it in turns to shovel up the soiled straw and wheelbarrow it out to the muck heap at the top of the field, while the other spread clean bedding. Then there were haynets to fill, sticky messes of molasses and bran to mix, buckets to wash and yards to sweep.

Not to mention feeding Speckle, Socks, the rabbits, the geese, the hens . . .

But the jobs seemed to get easier as the days grew lighter. By the beginning of March, Helen no longer had to wrap up in three jumpers just to take the treat of a juicy carrot out to Solo. And Hannah could carry fresh water into the barn without having first to unfreeze the tap in the yard.

'Spring's on its way!' their neighbour, Fred Hunt, called over the wall as he herded his cows down the lane.

An icy wind still blew down Doveton Fell and there was frost on the bare branches of the giant horse chestnut tree that overhung the yard. 'You could've fooled me!' Hannah murmured with a big shiver.

But of course there were lambs in the lakeside fields belonging to John Fox and green daffodil shoots, standing proud above last year's rotting leaves, in the beech-wood by the shore.

And as Easter approached the tourists returned

and business grew brisk in their mum's café. One Saturday in the middle of March, Mary Moore decided she needed some extra help and asked the twins to drive to Nesfield with her.

Hannah and Helen liked to work in The Curlew. The smell of coffee, fresh scones, toast and cakes wafted warmly around them as they busily collected dirty plates and stacked them in the dishwasher. They loved the tinkle of the bell when customers walked in and the sight of the town's busy main square through the window.

'Here comes Mandy Steele!' Helen pointed out to Hannah as they both wiped tables in a lull between customers.

The sight of the young farmer's wife reminded them of the very thing they'd been trying not to think about for the past month.

Trying but failing, as a matter of fact . . .

'If – *IF* we could choose between Toby, Tess and Titch, which one would you have?' Helen would ask dreamily, all their jobs for the day completed, lying with her arms behind her head, looking out of the bedroom window.

Hannah would think hard. She remembered that

Titch was the shyest, Tess the friendliest and Toby the most adventurous. 'That's really hard,' she would reply. 'Toby, I think.'

'Me too.' Helen had fallen in love with the tiny speckled adventurer.

'Wouldn't Speckle just love it if Toby came to live with us!' Hannah would sigh.

There was nothing that they could do except dream.

So, when Mandy Steele walked towards The Curlew pushing her bike, the twins were torn between running out to bombard her with questions and staying quietly in the background. After all, hearing news about the pups would only make them wish even harder that they could become Toby's proud owners.

They watched Mandy prop her bike against the lamppost and enter the café. Their mum came out from the kitchen at the sound of the doorbell.

'Good to see you!' Mary greeted the young woman and sat her down. 'Let me take your coat. What would you like – your usual pot of tea?'

Mandy relaxed. 'Whoo, do I need a hot drink! I've dashed from the bank to the decorating shop, and from there to see the electrician, until I don't know whether I'm coming or going!'

'The girls and I know what it's like.' Helen and Hannah's mum drew them into the conversation. 'Home Farm was a complete wreck when we took it over. Nothing worked – no water, no electricity. The walls were running with damp and there was no central heating. But at least we didn't have to try and run a sheep farm at the same time as getting the house in order.'

Hovering by Mandy's table, the twins nodded.

'How are the puppies?' Hannah asked shyly. She'd tried not to pop the question, but it seemed to escape anyway.

'The puppies are fine!' Mandy announced. 'They're driving us crazy, but they're fit as fiddles. Which is more than I can say for their poor mother.'

'Oh?' Mary asked with a look of concern.

Hannah and Helen sat down at Mandy's table and listened anxiously.

'Leila's sick, I'm afraid. Did you know that her milk was drying up last time you called?'

Helen nodded. She bit her lip as Mandy went on.

'Well, soon afterwards she had to give up feeding

altogether. We had to hand-rear the puppies until they could be weaned on to solid food. Meanwhile, Leila seemed to go downhill generally. So last week we called in the vet.'

'Sally Freeman?' Mary asked.

'Yes. She was up at our place checking on one of the ewes who was late delivering her twin lambs. So she came in and examined Leila. It turns out that the poor dog is suffering from a kidney complaint which means she's not producing enough sodium – well, without going into too much detail, Leila needs sodium tablets plus complete rest.'

'Which she won't get if she has to look after three mischievous puppies,' Mary said thoughtfully.

Helen and Hannah frowned. Leila's illness sounded serious.

'You're right.' Mandy agreed with the twins' mum. She took a grateful gulp of tea, then shook her head. 'The little rascals won't leave Leila alone, even though they're weaned. They're at the stage of wanting to play all day long, but not quite old enough to be separated from each other and sent off to different homes. We need to have them vaccinated and wormed – all that kind of thing –

before we stick an advert in the local paper.'

Hannah looked from Mandy to her still-thoughtful mum. Then, seeing that Helen was about to open her big mouth as usual, she fumbled for her foot under the table and stomped hard.

'Ouch!' Helen mouthed, looking as if she was in agony.

'How long before the pups can go off to new homes?' Mary asked Mandy quietly.

New customers came into the café and sat down near the window.

'A couple of weeks. Certainly by April,' Mandy replied.

'But that's two weeks too long for poor old Leila?' Mary turned, preparing to to serve her customers.

Mandy nodded. 'It's a big problem, huh?'

The twins's mum gave a brisk shake of her head. 'Not if you can find someone who'd be willing to take the puppies off your hands for a while.'

'Why, are you offering?' Mandy smiled at her own feeble attempt at a joke. Deep down she looked sad and worried.

Hannah and Helen stared at one then the other,

like spectators at a tennis match. Slowly their mouths
fell open.

'I certainly am,' Mary replied in a firm voice. 'I'd
like to help you out of a tough spot. And it goes
without saying that Helen and Hannah would be
delighted to look after Toby, Tess and Titch!'

'Only for two weeks, and not inside the house!' their
mum made them promise as she set off for work
next day.

'Mum, you're an angel!' Helen still couldn't believe
it. Less than twenty-four hours after the offer to
Mandy Steele, she and Hannah were sitting on the
gate at Home Farm, waiting for the Steeles' Land
Rover to arrive.

'Huh!' Mary shrugged off the compliments. 'I
know all too well what it must be like over at Keld
House. Pregnant ewes everywhere, lambs being
born, lack of sleep, tired, aching muscles . . .'

'We still think you're an angel for offering,'
Hannah insisted. She hadn't stopped smiling for an
entire day. All the time Helen and she had been
clearing out a corner of the barn ready for the new
arrivals, she'd been grinning from ear to ear.

Their mum paused a while longer before she got into the car. 'Repeat after me: "We will not get too attached to these puppies!" '

' "We . . ." ' Helen began.

' "Will not . . ." ' Hannah went on.

' "Get too . . ." '

' "Attached . . ." '

' "To these puppies!" ' they chanted together.

'Cross your hearts?' Mary insisted, the corners of her mouth twitching into a faint smile.

Hannah and Helen looked deadly serious on their gate-top perch. 'Cross our hearts!' they swore.

Their dad had overheard as he crossed the yard. 'That's like asking them not to breathe!' he warned Mary. 'Just wait until you see the pups, then you'll understand why!'

'We'll house train them for you,' Hannah promised Mandy. 'We'll keep them clean and feed them up with all the proper puppy foods!'

'And brush them and make sure they're warm at night,' Helen went on, feeling the flutter of excitement in her stomach as Mandy lifted a large cardboard box from her Land Rover.

'Come and see the cosy home we've made for them in the stable,' Hannah invited. She noticed Speckle sitting on the doorstep, head cocked to one side, looking curious about the big box and what was inside. 'Here, boy!' she called, and the dog trotted willingly to join them.

'Speckle's going to love this!' Smiling happily, Helen led the way into the barn.

Nosily Solo poked his dappled grey head over his stall door. Beyond him, Stevie gave a bad tempered '*Ee-aw*.' The donkey made it plain that he didn't like having his breakfast of sweet hay interrupted.

But the twins ignored him and took Mandy Steele to an empty stall at the far corner of the barn.

'Luke Martin gave us a wooden box which used to have oranges in it,' Helen told Mandy, who lowered her precious cargo to the floor. Straight away Speckle sniffed it and wagged his tail. One of the pups yelped and he barked back.

'We lined it with straw to make it soft, then covered the straw with a nice blanket.' Hannah explained how they'd made a cosy bed. 'We thought they should all sleep together for company.'

'Quite right.' Mandy made it clear that she

approved of the puppy hotel. Dipping into the cardboard box, she gently lifted the pups out and placed them in the converted orange crate. Soon Toby, Tess and Titch were blinking up at them from the middle of a soft blue blanket.

'They've grown!' Hannah gasped at the shiny-haired triplets.

Eagerly Speckle pushed through three pairs of legs to get his first clear sight of the puppies. He wagged his tail so hard that the white tip was just a blur.

'Look, there's a special light.' Helen flicked a switch and a dim bulb shone. 'It heats the stall as well as giving light. Mr Hunt uses it with calves when they're first born, so we borrowed it from him to keep the puppies warm at night.'

'That's great.' Mandy smiled down at Leila and Speckle's offspring. They stared back up, their huge eyes glinting in the dim overhead light.

Turning to go, she looked as if a big load had been taken off her shoulders. 'Thank you so much, girls. I honestly feel I can leave the puppies with you and not worry about them one little bit.'

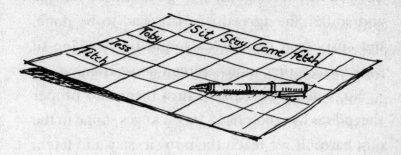

Four

'The thing is, we have to train them!' Helen declared.

Mandy Steele had left Titch, Tess and Toby in Helen and Hannah's capable care. She'd driven back to Keld House to look after Leila and two orphaned day-old lambs which Jack had brought into the kitchen to be hand-reared.

Now the girls watched the three pups snuggle deep into their new bed and settle down for an afternoon snooze. With ears flopped over their eyes and heads resting on their round paws, they looked peaceful and content.

'What do you mean exactly – "train them"?' Hannah asked, screwing up her mouth doubtfully.

39

'Do you mean, teach them to go to the loo outside and stuff?' She agreed that this had to be done, but suspected that Helen might be thinking of something more ambitious than house-training.

'No, I mean we have to turn them into proper sheepdogs like their dad!' Helen's eyes shone in the dim barn. 'If we teach them to sit, stay and fetch, Mandy and Jack will easily be able to find good homes for them in the farms around Doveton and Silcott!'

'Oh yeah, we teach them to herd sheep just like that!' Hannah remembered all the hard work they'd put into training Speckle when he'd first arrived, getting him to sit when they told him, then to come, stay and fetch. And Speckle had been a real Border collie, not a crossbreed.

'We did it before!' Helen insisted. 'The farmers said we'd never make a good working sheepdog out of Speckle when we rescued him from the stone quarry, and now look – he's a champion!'

Still sitting quietly beside the puppies' stall, Speckle heard Helen mention his name. His head and ears went up as he basked in her praise.

'But these pups are only twelve weeks old,'

Hannah reminded her. 'Speckle was about nine months. And there was only one of him, not three!'

Helen frowned, then thought of the one thing that would bring Hannah round to the training idea. 'OK, if you don't want to help, I'll do it by myself.'

'No way!' Hannah almost jumped down her throat. They never did anything by themselves – they were twins, they shared everything. 'If you're gonna teach the pups commands, so am I!'

'Great!' Now that they'd got the argument out of the way, Helen grew brisk. 'If Mum means what she says about only keeping Toby, Tess and Titch for two weeks, we don't have much time. So we'll need a training programme – a kind of chart of what we plan to teach them each day.

'We need columns, with a name at the top of each column. Then we'll have tasks like "Sit!" and "Stay!" down the left hand side of the page. We draw lines across to make boxes, and we tick a box each time one of the puppies learns to follow a command . . .' Running out of breath, she paused to let Hannah get a word in edgeways.

'When do we start?' she asked nervously, still not convinced that the plan would work.

41

'How about now?' Helen asked.

But Hannah leaned over the crate. 'They're fast asleep,' she pointed out. 'We can't wake the poor things up.'

'Hmm.' Helen took the point. So she turned on her heel and headed for the door. 'OK, let's go!' she decided. 'You grab a pen and a ruler, I'll find a nice big piece of paper. 'While the puppies are asleep, we can make the chart. Come on, Hann, what are you waiting for?'

Helen chewed the end of Hannah's pen. She was concentrating hard, thinking of things to add to the list of commands. She'd already included 'Sit!', 'Stay!', 'Come!' and 'Fetch!', but she still had two empty spaces at the bottom of the chart. 'Can you remember how John Fox makes Ben drive sheep in a straight line then turn them and bring them back down the hill?' she asked.

Hannah shook her head. She still thought this was way too advanced for the three little puppies. She sat opposite Helen at the kitchen table, one eye on the barn door which she could see through the window.

'I've got it!' Suddenly Helen remembered the shepherd's commands. 'You say "Steady!" to keep them going straight, and "Come by!" to bring them back.'

Hannah was only half listening. As Helen eagerly filled the two empty boxes, she saw the barn door fly open and Speckle come charging across the yard. Before she knew it, he was at the kitchen door, barking to be let in.

'Oh no!' Hannah jumped to her feet. 'Something's wrong!'

She ran to the door and opened it.

Seeing her there, Speckle turned and took two steps back across the yard. Then he bounded towards Hannah and barked again.

'He wants me to follow,' Hannah called. 'What is it, Speckle? What's happened?'

'Hang on, wait for me!' Helen put down the pen and ran to catch up. She saw Hannah and Speckle vanish into the barn and tried to prepare herself for what they might find.

Maybe she and Hannah had left the stall door open and the pups had climbed out of their crate and escaped. Maybe one had strayed into Stevie or Solo's

43

stall and got trampled on by a big, heavy hoof . . .
With her heart in her mouth, she joined Hannah and
Speckle by the puppies' makeshift bed.

'Look at this!' Hannah cried.

Gone was the cosy, peaceful scene which they'd
left fifteen minutes earlier. The pups must have
finished their nap and set about wrecking their bed.
The blue blanket had been dragged out of the crate
and now trailed across the floor. Then the pups had
turfed out the straw lining, scattering it far and wide.
Now, this very second, they were tumbling and
rolling, play-fighting their way round their stall.

'Toby!' Hannah watched him jump from the top
rim of the crate and land on Titch's back. The little
brown-and-black puppy yelped, then squeezed out
from underneath.

Meanwhile, Speckle jumped into the stall and set
about bringing back order to the scene.

First he grabbed Toby by the scruff of the neck.
He lifted him clean off the ground, carried him to
the crate and dumped him inside. *Thud!* Then he
turned and went to fetch Titch. *Thud!* Puppy number
two joined Toby.

'Where's Tess?' Helen murmured, half wanting to

smile at the cross look on Speckle's face. As soon as the pups' dad went looking for number three, Toby and Titch quickly scrambled out of the crate and took up their play-fight where they'd left off.

Speckle found Tess under a pile of straw and dumped her back in bed. *Thud!* Seeing that the crate was empty again, he growled and went in search of the missing duo. *Thud! Thud!* Each time he grabbed them a little more roughly and dumped them harder into the box.

Then, by the time his back was turned, all three pups had piggy-backed and scrambled their way out once more.

'I see your problem!' Hannah grinned.

Speckle looked worn out. He came to sit by the stall door, tongue lolling and breathing hard. These puppies were too much of a handful for him to deal with by himself, thank you very much.

'You need help!' Helen decided.

Tess, Titch and Toby tumbled in the straw and wrestled with their nice new blanket. Tess ran to hide behind the crate as Helen approached.

'Come here, you little rascal!' Helen scooped her up and scolded her softly. 'You should do as your dad tells you and stay in bed.'

Tess wriggled, her little legs paddling in mid-air.

Helen put her down on the few wisps of straw left in the crate. 'Stay!' she said firmly.

Tess looked up at her with big, soft brown eyes.

'Don't look at me like that!' Helen laughed. 'When I say "Stay", I mean "Stay"!'

'You sound like Dad,' Hannah told her, quickly gathering Toby and Titch and putting them in the box alongside Tess. 'Stay!' she said in a deep, firm voice.

The three puppies sat in a row, whining softly.

'Stay!' Helen insisted.

They hung their heads and sighed, making no effort to escape again.

'See!' Helen cried, dusting off her hands and turning away. 'Stay! That's one word they've learned already!'

She strode towards the door, past a curious Solo and cross-looking Stevie.

'Erm, Helen!' Hannah called her back. 'I don't think they heard you!'

A small black-and-white head and two grey-spotted paws had appeared under the stall door.

'For goodness sake!' Helen ran to look. She found Toby trying to squeeze and wriggle his way into the outside world, while Titch and Tess scampered and rolled at their dad's feet.

Hannah's mouth twitched. 'Like you said, he's a little rascal,' she grinned. 'And I reckon he's still got an awful lot to learn!'

'Girls, come quick! The pups have gone missing!'

'Hey, who let these puppies into the house?'

'Titch, leave the tea towel alone. Tess, drop it! Toby that's my slipper!'

'Helen, Hannah, these pups are driving us crazy!'

Not just once, but fifty times the cry went up.

'Sorry, Mum. Sorry, Dad!' Helen and Hannah scurried around all that Sunday afternoon and evening, trying in vain to prevent the next puppy disaster.

Every time they rounded the little dogs up and took them back to the barn, the girls would order them to stay.

'Stay!' Helen said in her severest voice, wagging her finger at sweet, shy little Tess.

'S-T-A-Y!' Hannah spelled it out for cheeky Titch

and bold Toby. 'That means, don't move!'

Ten seconds later, the pups would be gone.

'How does the idea of hitting your heads against a brick wall strike you?' their dad inquired with a wry grin.

'It sounds great!' Hannah groaned. 'Anyway, a whole lot better than Helen's crazy idea of training these three to be sheepdogs!'

It was last thing at night. The barn was locked and bolted, the puppies safe until tomorrow – she hoped!

'Well, get some sleep,' their dad told them both. 'You've got school in the morning, so you need your rest.'

'Fat chance!' Hannah sighed as her dad turned off the light. 'Toby, Titch and Tess will see to that!'

'Stay!' Helen growled for the hundredth time. It was half past eight and she hadn't even managed to have breakfast yet.

Toby was the worst puppy of all for disobeying the command. He was out of the crate and hightailing it towards the barn door before she could turn round.

49

'Hurry up, Helen!' Hannah appeared in the doorway, already dressed in school uniform. 'We're gonna be late!'

Helen made a grab for Toby as he dashed past. She missed and watched him squeeze under the partition into Stevie's stall. The donkey's hooves clattered against the stone floor and Stevie let out a screeching '*Ee-aw*' – *Get this clown out of here!*

Toby yelped and shot back under the barrier. He was still in one piece, but he looked shaken by the near miss.

'Serves you right,' Helen muttered, putting Toby back in the crate once more. 'Now, stay!'

'He won't!' Hannah predicted airily. 'I bet you a million pounds he never learns one single command the way you're trying to teach him!'

Helen gave up. The best she could do for now would be to lock and bolt the barn, then get their dad to check on the pups while she and Hannah were away at school. 'If you're so clever,' she muttered, 'you think of a better way.'

Hannah frowned. As she glanced at super-obedient Speckle sitting quietly by the kitchen door, a sudden thought struck her. If only they could teach the puppies to be as clever, sensible and useful as their dad. If only . . .

She turned to Helen and took up the challenge. 'Right,' she said, 'I will!'

Five

'OK, Speckle, I want you to show Toby, Tess and Titch how it's done!' Out in the field behind Home Farm, Hannah got ready to show Helen her brilliant idea.

It was after school on Monday and dusk was already falling on Doveton Fell. Still, Hannah was eager to prove that her method would work.

She made sure that Helen was in control of the three mischievous puppies. Sure enough, they were perched on the stone wall, their little tails wagging, ears cocked.

'Now watch this!' Hannah told them. Then she walked with Speckle across the field.

'Sit!' she told him in a firm voice.

Speckle sat.

'Stay!' she ordered, walking quickly ahead.

Speckle stayed.

'Here, boy!' Hannah called.

The obedient dog trotted briskly to join her.

Hannah took an old tennis ball from her pocket and threw it up the field. 'Fetch!' she cried.

Speckle streaked off to retrieve the ball. He brought it back and dropped it neatly at her feet.

Hannah picked it up again. 'See!' she said to Toby, Tess and Titch, 'That's all there is to it!'

'What was the point of that?' Helen wanted to know, as soon as they were back inside the barn. The puppy's special lamp glowed over their remade bed and they were curled up snugly, ready for a good night's sleep.

'Don't you get it? That was my new, super-quick method of training puppies!' Hannah was pleased with the demonstration. 'Now that they've seen how to do it properly, all they have to do is copy Speckle!'

Helen glanced down at the Border collie. 'So he's their role model?'

'That's right!' Who better for the pups to learn from than their champion sheepdog dad? Hannah had high hopes. 'I think we should get up early in the morning, put Speckle through his paces one more time, then get the pups to copy exactly what he does!'

'I'm f-f-freeezing!' Helen moaned.

Morning frost had turned the whole fell glistening white. The sky above was a clear, pale blue.

Buttoned up inside Helen's big jacket, Titch, Tess and Toby snuggled together for warmth.

'Stop complaining!' Hannah yelled. She was running down the field towards them, having worked for five minutes with Speckle. 'Could they see properly?' she demanded.

'Yeah, yeah!' As usual, Speckle had performed perfectly. Helen delved into her jacket and drew Toby out. He shivered as the cold air hit him, then tried to worm his way back into the warmth.

'No, you don't – it's your turn!' Hannah seized him and strode off. 'Watch this!' she told Helen, plonking Toby down on the frosty grass alongside Speckle. 'OK, that's "Sit"!'

Brr! Toby squatted on the ice-cold ground.

'Good boy! Ready, Speckle?' Hannah demanded.

Head up, ears alert, he showed that he was.

'Stay!' Hannah ordered, then walked away.

Speckle stayed. But Toby had already had enough of the mysterious new game. He launched himself across the field, yelping and tumbling, ducking and diving, covering himself from head to foot in the strange, sparkling white dust.

'*Stay!*' Hannah repeated the order. 'Toby, look at Speckle. Do what he does!'

From the wall top, Helen began to smile. She watched Toby career madly around the field, kicking up frost. He yapped and changed course, made straight for Hannah, grabbed the hem of her trouser-leg with his tiny teeth and wrestled her foot for all he was worth.

'Let go!' Hannah cried. 'Sit, Toby! You hear me – Stay!'

'Do you give up?' Helen laughed, watching the puppy roll away from Hannah's leg, pick himself up and head for the open gate which led into the lane.

'No. But don't just sit there, stop him!' Hannah

cried crossly. 'If we're not careful he could get squished by a car!'

As luck would have it, Toby's bolt for freedom put him on a collision course with Fred Hunt, who was driving a cartload of manure out of his farm gate. Now it seemed that Hannah's warning was about to come true.

'Watch out, Mr Hunt!' Helen jumped down from the wall, careful to keep a firm hold of Titch and Tess. Close behind her came Speckle and Hannah. They all ran as fast as they could to cut Toby off before he ran under the tractor's wheels.

The farmer saw them. But the sound of Helen's voice was drowned out by the engine, so he carried on crawling up the lane with his smelly load.

'Stop!' Helen yelled.

Toby sprinted ahead of her, ears flapping, the white tip of his tail bobbing down the narrow road.

'Stay, Toby!' Hannah screeched, her heart in her mouth.

But it was hopeless – the tiny runaway ignored her and headed full speed for the giant wheels.

Until, that is, Speckle put on a burst of speed. He sprinted ahead of Hannah and then Helen, barking at the top of his voice. At last, Fred Hunt understood that they wanted him to halt.

It was almost too late. Fred slammed on the brakes at the very moment when Toby reached the tractor. As the puppy squeezed into the gap between the machine and the wall, the cartload of manure shuddered to a halt. The cart rocked from side to side, spilling the top layer of its slippery contents on to the lane.

Splat! A big blob of cow dung dropped on to Toby.

'Oh yuck!' Helen cried, slowing down to let Hannah run ahead and rescue him.

Fred looked down the side of his tractor, saw what had happened, then tipped his cap to the back of his head, grinning at the puppy's plight. 'There's nothing wrong with a drop of muck,' he reassured Hannah, who gingerly squeezed by the cart.

'I dever said dere was!' she replied, trying not to breathe through her nose.

'Looks like the little scamp escaped without a scratch.' The farmer waited for her to pick Toby up and step clear. Then his grin changed to a puzzled frown. 'Hang on, I thought your mum and dad had said no to more animals at Home Farm!'

Pooh! Hannah held the smelly puppy at arm's length. 'Dey hab,' she agreed. 'Dis pubby isn't ours . . .'

As she ran out of breath, Helen stepped in to explain. 'That's Toby, and this is Titch and Tess. We're looking after them for two weeks and training them to grow up to be sheepdogs like Speckle.'

Even as she said it, she realised how stupid this must seem.

Fred stared at two wimpy little mongrels shivering inside her jacket and at the third all covered in cow muck. 'Nay,' he said with a doubtful shake of the head. 'You've as much chance of turning them three into working dogs as I do of winning the lottery!'

'Don't listen to Fred!' Hannah told the puppies. She was giving them a pep talk before taking them out to the field again. 'Just because you're little and don't look as if you'll ever be big and strong like Speckle doesn't mean you won't be good sheepdogs when you grow up!'

Titch, Toby and Tess lined up in the yard. They yawned and stretched after their day spent playing and snoozing in the barn while the twins had been to school. When a handful of straw blew by, Toby pounced.

Just then, Mary Moore arrived home from work. 'More training?' she asked Hannah as she got out of the car. She passed Toby, who was still chasing the scattering wisps. 'Pooh, someone needs a bath!' she remarked.

'That's cow muck from this morning,' Helen chipped in from the barn door. She was hanging back from this latest training session, finding excuses not to go out on to the field.

'There's nothing wrong with a drop of muck!' Mary said in Fred Hunt's deep voice.

Hannah tutted. 'You lot can mock all you want, but Speckle and I have work to do.'

' "Sit!", "Stay!", "Come here!" ' Helen teased. 'Hey, Hann, when d'you reckon we'll be able to tick one of our boxes?'

'Soon!' Hannah said through gritted teeth, picking up Titch and Tess. 'Stay!' she said to Toby and Speckle in her firmest voice.

'Fat chance!' Helen laughed.

The little black-and-white pup charged after the straw and vanished under their mum's parked car. He came out the far side and began to scramble up the rough surface of the farmyard wall. Soon he had climbed, to the top and was balancing like a tightrope walker and heading towards the barn.

'I daren't look!' Helen grimaced.

'He's a little dare-devil!' Mary enjoyed Toby's latest adventure. 'David, come out and look at this!'

Helen and Hannah's dad emerged from the house with lengths of recently developed film strung round his neck. 'What? Where?' he mumbled.

'On the wall, by the water trough – Oops!'

Everyone gasped as Toby missed his footing and almost fell. Speckle gave a sharp bark, as if warning the pup to stop fooling around.

But Toby ignored them all. He looked down and saw the trough, spotted his own image reflected in the smooth surface. The sight seemed to fascinate him, as he stopped and stared.

'Uh-oh!' Helen was the first to guess what was about to happen. 'Toby has this thing about water, remember!'

The puppy craned forward for a better view of the shiny surface. He saw another dog, just like him.

He liked what he saw and leaned even further forward.

'Watch out!' Helen yelled, but it was too late.

Toby had lost his balance and was toppling head-first. There was a splash as he disappeared from view.

'Speckle, fetch!' Helen cried.

The clever dog reacted quick as a flash. He darted for the stone trough and jumped up to rest his front paws against the side. By the time Toby floated to the surface, he was ready.

Gulp-splutter! The puppy swallowed water then coughed it up. He held his tiny head and the tip of his nose above the surface, doing a frantic doggy paddle to stay afloat.

Speckle judged it right, waiting for Toby to struggle towards him before he leaned over and grabbed him by the scruff. Then he dragged him from the water, swinging him out of the trough and dumping him on dry land.

'He looks like a drowned rat,' David commented, turning back into the house to answer the phone.

'Poor Toby!' Hannah cried, running to wrap him in her jacket before he froze.

'I know he needed a bath, but he could've waited!'

Helen grinned. It seemed there was no end to the trouble Toby got into.

Hannah was fussing over him and Helen was telling Speckle what a good dog he was when their dad reappeared at the door. His face had turned serious and he stepped out hesitantly.

'Who was that on the phone?' their mum asked.

'Jack Steele,' he murmured. 'He was asking after the pups.'

'I hope you told him we were managing fine,' Hannah cut in. No way did she want the Steeles to think that the puppies were more than she and Helen could handle.

'Hmm? Yes, no worries there,' her dad answered. 'But Jack did pass on a bit of rather worrying news.'

'About Leila?' Helen guessed. 'She's not getting worse!'

David frowned then nodded. His voice dropped. 'Jack tells me that she's very ill. They've had the vet again, and Sally says it really is touch and go.'

Six

The bad news about Leila worried Helen and Hannah more than they were prepared to admit.

They went about with sad faces, worried every time the phone rang that it might be Jack or Mandy Steele telling them that Leila hadn't made it.

'Cheer up,' their dad said, giving them a quick, understanding hug. 'Concentrate on training those pups – it will give you something useful to do.'

The girls sighed and took his advice. Every day, both before and after school, they took Toby, Titch and Tess into the field to watch Speckle, then follow his example. By Wednesday of that week, they felt sure that Titch and Tess were making progress.

'They understand "Sit!" and "Stay!",' Hannah told her mum after a teatime training session. She was busy putting ticks on the chart which she'd laid out on the floor. 'You should see them, Mum. They sit there and look so sweet, with Speckle beside them showing them what to do.'

Mary had spent the day at the café, serving hot drinks and healthy snacks to hikers brave enough to walk the fells in early spring. Now she was enjoying her favourite TV soap. 'Well done,' she murmured, when she heard that two of the pups were quick learners. 'But what about Toby?'

'Ah!' Helen cut in. She raised her eyebrows and shook her head. 'Hmm, Toby!'

'Talking of whom . . .' David strolled into the lounge and interrupted the conversation. 'I've just come in from the barn to ask you if either of you have seen young Toby recently.'

Hannah jumped up from the rug. 'Isn't he there?'

Her dad shook his head. 'I thought he might have snuck in here.'

'Uh-oh.' Helen could see another mad chase coming. Since Toby had charged at Fred Hunt's tractor, then taken the plunge into the water trough on Sunday, they'd had to get used to rescuing him from all sorts of sticky situations.

On Monday there'd been the climb-up-to-the-rafters crisis in the barn. Tuesday was the hide-in-the-boot-of-the-car routine. Earlier today there was the annoy-Stevie-then-run-away adventure. If Toby had been a kitten, Helen reckoned that he would've used up at least five of his nine lives already.

'He's not here.' Hannah ran to the kitchen to check. She'd been the one to climb up to the top of the barn and bring Toby down. Her legs had been like jelly as she'd edged along the stout beam, but she'd gritted her teeth and caught hold of him. He'd wriggled and squirmed in her grasp all the way back along the beam and down the ladder. As soon as she'd put him safely back in bed, he'd begun the whole thing over again.

'Once could be an accident!' their mum had grinned. 'But the same thing twice begins to look deliberate!'

These days, they panicked less. Toby could take care of himself, it seemed.

But still, Hannah and Helen didn't like him to go missing in the dark. So they put on their jackets and ran out to search the barn.

'I hope he didn't decide to annoy Stevie again,' Helen muttered.

The donkey had already made it plain that he liked to keep his stall to himself. And those hooves were hard and sharp when he lashed out with them.

'Or take a swim in the water trough.' Hannah paused to investigate. 'Nope. Well, that's a relief!'

They ran on into the barn to find both Solo and Stevie quietly munching hay from their nets.

'No sign of him here either,' Helen reported from the donkey's stall.

'Maybe Dad made a mistake.' Hannah decided to check the puppies' bed. Nope to that too – only Tess and Titch were snuggled up in the blue blanket.

'What now?' Helen asked helplessly. It was already pitch black out there. Finding one small puppy on a big black fellside was no joke.

But the answer came in the tramp of heavy feet across the farmyard.

'Hello, anybody there?' a gruff voice called.

Tramp-tramp – the feet approached the barn.

'Fred!' Helen ran to open the door and found him standing in shirtsleeves and fleece waistcoat.

'I saw the light on in here. I take it this is who you're looking for?'

Hannah joined Helen at the door in time to see their neighbour open up his waistcoat to reveal a black-and-white pup cowering inside.

'Toby!' Helen and Hannah cried.

Producing the runaway like a bad-tempered magician lifting a rabbit out of a hat, Fred Hunt presented Toby to Helen. 'He was in my cowshed annoying my prize heifer. I was eating my tea when I heard her kicking up a fuss. When I went out to see what it was all about, I found this little devil running at the poor girl's heels, yap-yapping and upsetting her no end.'

As he told the story, the old farmer shook Toby until his eyes popped.

'Thank you, Mr Hunt!' Helen said anxiously. She took the puppy from him. 'We're really sorry Toby was a nuisance.'

The old farmer sniffed. 'How long did you say you were looking after him for?'

'Two weeks. Well, one and a half now.' Hannah realised that annoying their neighbour was a bad idea. Farmers like Fred had a way of making their opinions felt, and it was always best to keep on their good sides. 'Honestly, Mr Hunt, we'll keep an eye on Toby and make sure it doesn't happen again.'

'Well, I'd do that if I were you.' Fred sniffed. Then he offered them a piece of advice. 'Better still, if I was your mum and dad, I'd send those useless pups packing, back to where they came from – no messing!'

'He's not, so he can't!' was Helen's secret response. Fred Hunt's verdict had half scared and half annoyed her. He'd made her more determined to work hard with Titch, Tess, and especially Toby, to turn them into respectable working dogs.

'He called them useless!' Hannah found it hard to forgive their grumpy neighbour. 'I'd like to know what use Fred Hunt was when he was three months old!'

Helen grinned. 'Yeah, wearing nappies and bawling!'

For the next few days, the girls went on grumbling about the cold-hearted farmer – criticising the way he'd shaken Toby until the puppy's eyes popped and then had had the nerve to offer them bad advice.

They made doubly sure not to let Toby slip away on one of his jaunts down to High Hartwell.

'Let's put an extra plank along the bottom of their stall door!' Hannah suggested, already armed with hammer and nails.

The banging upset Stevie, but it meant that the pups could no longer squeeze under the door and leg it down the lane.

'Yeah, and let's fix a chicken-wire roof about a metre off the ground, so they can't climb out!' Helen's brainwave was more complicated to carry out, but in the end they'd fixed a wonky wire roof into place. Now Toby, Tess and Titch could only come out when the girls decided it was time to exercise and train.

And they were pleased with the result. During the day, when they were at school, they need have no worries about the pups. Then, in the evenings, the three little bundles of energy would romp out in the field with Speckle, eager to please.

'Sit!' Helen would cry.

Tess and Titch would obey. Toby would tumble, roll and jump.

'Stay!' Hannah's command began to work on Titch

and Tess. But for Toby, life seemed too short to stay in one place.

By Saturday morning, the girls had ticked off more boxes for Titch and Tess. But Toby's column was still blank.

'Today's the day!' Hannah told the speckled pup, taking him out alone.

She and Helen had decided that it was time for a solo session. They ignored the fine drizzle that was drifting across the hillside and plonked Toby on the grass beside an ever-willing Speckle.

Toby looked up pleadingly at them through the cold rain, as if to ask what he'd done to deserve this.

'Toby, you have to learn the basic commands!' Helen told him sternly, though his big brown eyes were almost melting her heart. 'How can you grow up to be a proper sheepdog like Speckle if you ignore everything we say?'

The puppy whimpered and let his ears droop over his eyes.

'It's cold out here, let's get a move on.' Hannah hopped up and down to keep warm. As she glanced up the fell at the heavy grey clouds, she spotted a small white blob amongst the heather. 'What's that?' She pointed at the moving shape.

'It looks like a sheep or a lamb.' Helen couldn't quite make it out either. 'But what's it doing all the way up here?'

The land beyond their sloping field wasn't farmland, so any animal finding its way on to the upper fell must have escaped from one of the valley farms.

'It's lost!' By straining her eyes, Hannah grew certain that the moving speck was a lamb in need of rescue. So she forgot about Toby's training session and sent Speckle off to bring the stray lamb down from the fell.

'Fetch!' she told him.

The one word sent Speckle off at a fast lope. He leaped the wall and bounded on up the rocky slope.

'Steady!' Hannah called. She crossed her fingers – it was a long time since they'd asked Speckle to do any serious sheep herding. 'Let's hope he hasn't forgotten,' she murmured to Helen.

Speckle ran straight as an arrow towards the distant lamb. When he reached his target, he slowed

and circled round the far side, crouching low to await another command.

'Come by!' Hannah yelled, her hands cupped round her mouth so that the sound would carry.

Speckle heard. Still crouching, he edged never the lamb, forcing it down the hill towards Home Farm.

'Come by, Speckle!' Helen had picked Toby up and joined in the attempt to bring the lamb down. 'How brilliant is that!' she whispered, as their champion dog hustled and worried his quarry. 'You see!' she told the puppy. 'That's what being a sheepdog really means!'

By now, Speckle and the lamb were drawing near

and the lamb was starting to object to being driven through the gate into the field. She skittered to one side, only to find Speckle already cutting her off and driving her on. A second dart in the other direction brought the clever dog wheeling round the back and pushing her on again until she squeezed through the gate.

'Brilliant!' Hannah clapped, then took pity on the frightened lamb. She ran to help Speckle corner her, darting forward to gather the spindly creature in her arms.

Moving in behind Hannah, Helen hung on to an excited Toby. She spotted a patch of blue dye on the lamb's back and quickly recognised the marking. 'Hey, that's one of John Fox's lambs. Come on, Hann, let's take her back home straight away!'

Seven

'Well done, girls!' John Fox's thin, normally serious face cracked into a wide smile. He'd come out of the house to greet them with his own sheepdog at his heels, and had gladly taken the stray lamb from Hannah.

'It wasn't us, it was Speckle,' she told the farmer. But the warm glow of a job well done still flushed her cheeks.

'Which means you should thank Ben too,' Helen pointed out, stooping to pat Mr Fox's dog. 'Because it was Ben who taught Speckle everything in the first place!'

They all smiled, then laughed at Toby, who was

tucked under Helen's arm and gave a jealous growl as she patted Ben.

The wise old dog cocked an ear, then decided to overlook the puppy's rude interruption.

'Anyhow, it was good of you to bother,' John Fox insisted. Dressed in a baggy checked jacket and flat cap, which was the colour of the peaty brown bog that bordered this stretch of Doveton Lake, he invited the twins in to drink orange juice and eat chocolate biscuits.

'Leave the pup in the yard with Ben and Speckle,' he suggested. 'They'll look after him and see he doesn't come to any harm.'

Helen hesitated, then did as John asked. She knew that like a lot of the farmers round here, he had a no-dogs-in-the-house rule. 'Be good!' she warned Toby, who just stared back up at her with his big, gleaming eyes.

They were two bites in to their second chocolate digestive when the triumphant visit to Lakeside Farm turned sour.

Through the open door of the kitchen came a wild yapping (Toby), followed by two tones of gruff bark (Ben and Speckle), followed by a small sploosh and two big ones.

Sploosh! SPLOOSH! SPLOOSH!

'Toby!' Helen and Hannah shot out of their seats.

They should have thought about it sooner – Toby and water could only lead to one thing!

'What the . . . !' John Fox's creaky bones would only let him stand slowly. He watched Helen and Hannah make a beeline out of the door, across the yard and down to the edge of the lake.

They arrived to see the grown dogs swimming furiously towards Toby, who was gulping both air and water through his open mouth as he doggy-paddled in a small circle.

'Toby, come *here*!' Helen cried. *Not again!* she groaned to herself.

A speedboat out on the lake churned up the smooth surface and sent a wave of water in their direction.

The puppy rocked in the wash from the boat and his head disappeared under the surface.

'Fetch, Ben! Fetch, Speckle!' Hannah cried, her voice cracked with alarm. Taking the plunge into a small water trough was one thing. Diving into a huge lake was another.

The two dogs closed in on the spot where the puppy had gone under. They dived down and it was Ben who came up holding Toby by the scruff of the neck.

Then Mr Fox arrived on the scene. 'That was a close shave,' he commented drily. 'If that had happened in other stretches of the bank, like that jetty for instance, that pup might have been pulled down by the strong current. He'd have had no chance of being rescued!'

Hannah glanced along the bank to a smartly painted wooden pier that ran out at right angles to the shore. There were two rowing-boats tied to it, and a red-and-white lifebelt attached to a post. She shivered as she realised that reckless Toby had just used up another cat life.

'Come by!' Helen called to Ben and Speckle, wondering if the same rules applied to dogs in water as on dry land. Anyway, it seemed to work, as the two collies headed straight for the bank.

After thirty seconds of strong swimming, Ben was able to drop one bedraggled puppy at the twins' feet.

'Hm, that'll teach him not to go charging into lakes

if he can't swim,' John Fox commented, taking care to stand out of the way as Speckle and Ben shook themselves dry.

Hannah picked Toby up and got showered. 'I doubt it,' she sighed.

Nothing so far – not soakings, not narrow escapes from tractors, nor near misses from flying hooves or death-defying climbs into the rafters, had taught the scatterbrained, speckled puppy the least little scrap of common sense.

'While you're here, how about putting Speckle to his proper use?' John Fox asked in his dry way.

By 'proper use' the farmer obviously meant getting the sheepdog to herd sheep.

Helen hesitated. Maybe they shouldn't push their luck as far as Toby was concerned. If they stayed any longer at Lakeside Farm, then perhaps the near miss would turn into true disaster.

But Hannah was eager for Speckle to work with Ben, his old master. 'What do you want him to do?' she asked.

John walked them from the water's edge, up a gradually sloping field to a small fold containing fifty or so ewes and lambs. 'I need to move these to the top field,' he told them. 'The tricky bit is where we come out of this low field on to the road and we have to drive them thirty yards to the next gateway.'

Hannah and Helen saw the stretch of lane, bordered by high stone walls. They saw immediately that it would help John to have two dogs working – one to stand guard at the far end so the sheep didn't push beyond the gateway, and another to drive them along from behind.

So they let the farmer put Speckle to work with Ben, watching proudly as their own dog joined the professional.

John whistled a high, long note – a signal for the dogs to wade in amongst the sheep in the fold and start driving them out.

The ewes and lambs bleated crossly, jostling together, then blindly bursting out from the stone pen. They made a run to one side until Ben shot out and steered them straight.

'Steady!' John called to Speckle.

The twins' dog kept low and drove the last sheep from the fold.

Then they were all out and running across the

low field, flanked by the two dogs, who seemed to work like clockwork at their task.

'You see!' Helen held Toby up to give him a good view. 'Wouldn't you like to do that? Yes, you would!'

Toby snuffled her hand and wriggled.

'C'mon!' Hannah said impatiently. 'They've already got as far as the lane!'

As John Fox walked stiffly after the flock, resting heavily on his long stick and grumbling about his bad rheumatism, Helen and Hannah overtook him.

'See, it doesn't matter if Mr Fox is on the spot or not,' Helen explained to Toby. 'Ben and Speckle have already got their orders to hold the sheep at this gate and not let them out into the road until we arrive to open the gate.'

The puppy took a look and seemed for a moment to understand. He stopped squirming and looked hard at the crouching dogs and restless sheep.

'*Yap-yap-yap!*' he shrilled suddenly.

A sheep at the front of the bunch spooked and leaned hard against the wooden gate that led into the lane.

'*Yap-yap-yap-yap-yap-YAP!*' Toby's high bark split the quiet air.

Two more sheep leaned against the gate until it broke from its hinges. *Crack!* The old wood split and the barrier fell to the ground.

'*Stampede!*' Hannah breathed in horror as the sheep set off up the lane. She pictured a car coming round the bend, meeting up with fifty loose sheep. Worse still, someone on a bicycle or on foot.

'Can't you shut that dog up?' John Fox yelled as he strode past Helen. He whistled urgently at Ben, who cut round the tail-end of the herd and streaked up the side of the field for fifty metres, then swerved suddenly, jumped over the wall and came out on the lane ahead of the leading runaway.

Seeing the way blocked, the sheep dug in its heels and stopped.

Meanwhile, Speckle too seemed to realise what was needed. He stayed behind, rounding up the tail-enders and pushing them out into the lane. As soon as he had the last lamb out of the field, he crouched by the broken gate and barred their way back in.

Now, with Ben at the front and Speckle behind, the two dogs had the situation under control.

'Come by!' Mr Fox called, with another whistle.

Ben forced the ringleaders back down the lane

until they came level with the gate they needed to take.

'Run and open it!' the farmer yelled at Hannah. 'Your young legs are faster than mine!'

She raced to do as she was told, running up the field and opening the gate wide. In the lane, the sheep pushed and shoved purposelessly until one spied the new opening and made a break into the top field.

The others followed like woolly grey robots, with their lambs skipping happily behind.

Helen closed her eyes with relief. From down the hill she felt a deep shame for the damage Toby had caused and the narrowly escaped disaster. Tears pricked her eyelids as she gazed at the broken gate.

'Go on, take him away!' Once the crisis was over, Mr Fox turned to yell at her. He'd almost lost a quarter of his herd, thanks to Toby. 'I'd have thought you'd know better!'

Helen hung her head and began to trail off with Toby.

'We're sorry, Mr Fox.' Hannah tried her best to put things right before she called Speckle and they ran to catch up with Helen and Toby.

'Sorry's not enough,' the old farmer grumbled. He shot Hannah a sharp look from under the peak of his cap. 'This isn't the first time that little nuisance has caused bother, is it?'

'No. I – er –'

'That's right. I was talking to Fred Hunt, and he told me a couple of things. He said you two had some silly idea about training this litter.'

Hannah sighed. In the distance, she saw Helen making her dejected way along the water's edge towards the village, the disgrace of what had happened obviously weighing heavy on her shoulders. How could something that had begun so well go so badly wrong, she wondered.

'Do you want my advice?' John Fox muttered, his sharp gaze fixed on her blushing face.

No! she thought. *No!* She'd heard all this before and knew what was coming next.

The farmer gave it anyway. 'You should give up your daft plan and send the whole litter off to a dogs' home. Let them find owners who couldn't care less that the three little pests don't have a decent set of brain cells to share between them!'

Eight

The trouble with living in Doveton was that you could never keep anything quiet.

Even before Hannah, Helen and Toby had reached the village, word had got round about the puppy causing John Fox's sheep to stampede up the lane.

'I'd get the little scamp on a lead if I were you!' Luke Martin called from the doorway of his shop. He winked knowingly at Helen, who was still carrying Toby under one arm. 'I hear he has a habit of getting into serious trouble!'

Hannah sighed and shook her head. 'How did you know?'

'Bush telegraph!' Luke said cheerfully, before

disappearing inside to answer the phone.

'What on earth's a bush telegraph?' Helen frowned.

Hannah shrugged. 'Who cares?'

They hadn't gone fifty metres before Len Coates from Skrike Farm pulled up in his Land Rover and leaned out for a chat. 'Ah, so that's the famous pup! I expect you girls are at your wits' end, wondering what to do with the little pest!'

Helen tutted. 'Who told you?'

Len tapped the side of his nose with his forefinger. 'Word gets around,' he said mysteriously.

'What are people saying?' Hannah wanted to know.

Len grinned. 'Let's see. Basically, that the pup is an accident waiting to happen.'

Helen hitched Toby up so that he snuggled more tightly under her arm. Happy to be carried, he stayed close and wagged his stumpy tail.

'How can they say that?' Hannah pleaded. 'It's only because he's young and has a lot to learn. He's no more of a pest than any other puppy!'

'Try telling that to John Fox and Fred Hunt!' Len laughed as he pulled away from the kerb. 'If they had their way, they'd chase your Toby clean off the fell and into the next county!'

'What if they're right?' Helen was the first to admit her own doubts to Hannah as they cleaned out Solo and Stevie's stalls first thing next morning.

'They're not,' Hannah said stubbornly. She scooped droppings and soiled straw into the wheelbarrow, ready to push it out to the yard. 'It wasn't Toby's fault that he started to bark just at the wrong moment. How was he to know that it would set the sheep off in a stampede?'

Helen cut the twine on a new bale of straw. 'I know, Hann. But the fact is, Toby does have this habit of getting into trouble – much more than either Titch or Tess. And on top of that, he doesn't seem to learn anything.'

Taking a break from the scooping, Hannah breathed in deeply. It was true – Toby hadn't taken on board the order to 'Stay!', let alone 'Come here!' and 'Fetch!'. 'Maybe he's deaf,' she suggested weakly.

'Face it, Hann!' Helen shook her head. She pushed Solo to one side of the stall so that she could spread the clean straw.

'OK, then. He's just a bit more adventurous than the other two.' End of conversation. Hannah set up a tune inside her head so she didn't have to listen any more. Then she seized the wheelbarrow handles and began to trundle it out of the barn.

As she reached the yard, she saw a car pull up and Sally Freeman get out with her little son, Ashley.

The vet spotted Hannah and waved. 'I hear you're taking care of three puppies!' she called.

'Yes. What about it?' Hannah wasn't ready for another dose of unwanted, so-called expert advice, so she trundled on with her barrow.

'Nothing. I think it's very kind of you,' Sally said with a smile. 'Maybe you could take Ashley to see them. He likes puppies and kittens.'

'Oh!' Surprised, Hannah stopped in her tracks and blushed. 'Sorry, I didn't mean . . .' At last someone was being nice about Toby, Titch and Tess. 'Yeah, sure. C'mon, Ashley, I'll show you the pups!'

The little blond-haired boy ran with her into the barn while his mum called in the house for a cup of coffee with David Moore.

Ashley slowed down when he came to Solo's stall and the pony poked his head over the door.

'It's OK, he won't hurt you.' Helen's head appeared beside Solo's. 'He's gentle as anything.'

So four-year-old Ashley trotted on past Solo and then Stevie, who eyed him suspiciously but decided not to *ee-aw* at the top of his voice and frighten him out of his wits.

'Toby, Tess and Titch are in the stall in the corner.' Hannah urged Ashley to open the door and peep in. 'Mind they don't escape. What are they doing? Are they asleep?'

He nodded. 'I like the little black-and-brown one best. What's his name?'

'Titch. He's sweet, isn't he?' Through the narrow gap Hannah caught a glimpse of three snoozing pups – Tess and Toby lying side by side, with only Titch's little face peeping out from a deep fold in the blanket.

Ashley nodded. 'You're looking after them because their mum's sick, aren't you?'

'That's right. But we hope Leila will soon be better.' Hannah looked on the bright side for the little boy's sake.

He frowned and shook his head. 'My mum just went to see her. She's really, really sick.'

Hannah stared at him. 'You've just been to Keld

House to visit Leila?' The news startled her and brought Helen quickly out of Solo's stall.

'Let's go and see Sally,' Helen suggested. 'Find out exactly how Leila is.'

'Can I stay and watch the puppies?' Ashley wanted to know.

'You go. I'll stay here with Ashley,' Hannah told Helen, dreading what the vet might say.

So Helen dashed inside. When she came back, her face was pale, her mouth set in a grim line.

Hannah looked up and knew at once that what Ashley had said was true.

'Leila's definitely worse,' Helen told her. 'There's no change to her actual illness, but Sally says it looks as if she's given up the will to live.'

'It's a difficult thing to explain,' Sally Freeman said quietly. She drove carefully through Silcott village, knowing that Titch, Tess and Toby were sitting in the back with the twins and Ashley.

At first, news of the crisis at Keld House had stunned Helen and Hanah. They'd stayed in the barn, not knowing what to do or say.

'How come Leila doesn't want to get better?'

Hannah had said over and over.

Helen hadn't known the answer. All she had been able to think was that there must be something they could do.

'Maybe she's missing her puppies,' Ashley had suggested, his round, freckled face thoughtful.

The idea had floated in the dim light of the barn for ages.

Then Helen had seized on it. 'Of course!' she'd cried. 'Leila thinks she doesn't have a reason to live. But if we took Toby, Tess and Titch to Keld House, then she'd remember why she has to get better!'

And so it was because of Ashley that Helen and Hannah had arranged this visit.

First, they'd got Sally Freeman to agree that her little son might be right. 'If I was Leila, no matter how sick I was I'd want to see my pups!' Helen had argued, and the vet had accepted that it couldn't possibly do any harm.

Then they'd arranged for Sally to come back to Home Farm that afternoon and drive them all over to Keld House.

And now, here she was, answering the twins' questions about the mystery of Leila's illness.

'It's hard to know exactly what's going on,' she told them. A glance at her watch told her that it was coming up to half past three. 'Medically, Leila's condition is certainly serious. Kidney failure can cause death, but in this case, I think we got it under control just in time.'

'So she should be able to get better?' Hannah insisted. From her lap, Tess raised her head to sniff the interesting scents drifting in through the Land Rover window.

'In a strictly medical sense – yes. But with animals it's strange. We vets do all we can for them, but still there's the unknown factor of the patient's willpower. The animal must want very strongly to recover, otherwise, all the veterinary skill in the world won't make any difference.'

'OK.' Convinced that a visit from the pups would tip the balance, Helen was impatient to arrive. She looked out to see the sign for Silcott Farm – that meant there was still five minutes to go before they reached the Steeles' house. So she filled the time by checking that Ashley was happy nursing Titch on his lap and telling Toby that he had to be good.

'Extra, extra good!' Helen insisted. 'We don't want

96

to be chasing you when what we should be doing is helping Leila to get better.'

'Don't get your hopes up too high,' Sally warned as she drew up in the yard at Keld House. 'Leila is a very sick dog, remember.'

The reminder made them nervous when Jack Steele came to the door and let them in.

'Mandy told me to expect you,' he told them. 'But she's too upset to see you right now.'

'We're not too late? Leila isn't . . .?' Sally asked.

Jack shook his head. 'No, but it doesn't look good.' He led the train of visitors into the kitchen. 'Just a quick visit to see how the poor girl reacts,' he suggested. 'But don't expect too much.'

Leila lay in her basket by the stove, eyes closed, thin sides heaving slowly in and out. At first, Helen and Hannah thought she was sleeping, but as they tiptoed near, the sick dog opened her eyes. The look she gave them was dull and weary.

Hannah swallowed hard. She saw at a glance that the life was ebbing out of Leila. She knelt down by her side. 'Look!' she whispered, offering the dog a glimpse of Toby whom she held out in both hands.

Toby didn't struggle. He looked at his sick mother

with bright eyes, ears cocked and straining forward to be near her. When Hannah held him closer still, he put out his tongue to lick her whiskery face.

Leila didn't move. She felt the puppy's rough tongue and sighed. She closed her eyes and opened them again. Then she turned her head a fraction, put out her tongue and licked him back.

'Good!' Sally Freeman murmured. She told Ashley and Helen to move the two other puppies in close.

Now Titch and Tess crept forward to say hello. Leila turned her head again. They saw the tip of her long, bushy tail wag faintly.

'Good!' Sally said again. 'Hannah, keep an eye on Toby. See that he doesn't get too excited.'

'Easy!' Hannah murmured as the speckled puppy pushed in front of the other two.

Toby quietened down and pushed in close to Leila. He lifted a paw to touch her head, which she slowly raised above the edge of the basket. Now her tail was wagging harder and she was pushing with her legs to stand up.

'Should we let her?' Helen asked, afraid that Leila was too weak.

Sally nodded. 'Let her try.'

It was sad, the way the poor dog had to struggle to raise her body on her weak legs. Leila wobbled and shook, but she was determined to stand. Her three puppies watched and waited, giving small yaps of encouragement.

At last she made it. She trembled with the effort, but she'd done it.

'Good girl!' Jack Steele came forward and gathered Leila in his arms. He walked towards the hall, holding her close to his chest. Toby, Tess and Titch followed hard on his heels. They bundled after him into the hallway and romped around his feet as he called up the stairs.

'Mandy, come and look at this!' he cried. 'It's a miracle – the pups are here and Leila's back on her feet. It turns out the visit is working a treat!'

Nine

'Amazing!' Helen sat back and breathed a giant sigh of relief.

'Yeah!' Hannah was too choked to say more. She held Toby on her lap, hoping and praying that Leila really did stand a chance of getting better.

Sitting between the twins, on the back seat of his mum's car, Ashley beamed.

'Well done!' Sally praised them as she reversed the Land Rover into the lane. 'I'm sure that did a lot to stop Leila's downward slide. I also think it would be a good idea to repeat the visit as soon as possible.'

'Great!' Nothing would please Helen more. As she

looked out across the breezy, exposed slope of Skrike Fell, she looked forward to lots more drives out to the remote farmhouse.

'Hang on, Mum!' Ashley yelled suddenly.

Sally braked hard, churning up the loose gravel in the gateway.

They all turned to see Jack Steele running across the yard. When the vet opened her window, he leaned in to deliver a message.

'Sorry, Sally, I almost forgot. I promised Malcolm Altham, from Silcott Farm, that I'd ask you to drop in at his place after you'd finished here.'

Sally nodded. 'What's the problem?'

'Apparently he has a sick calf he'd like you to look at.'

'OK, thanks, Jack.'

'No. Thank *you*,' he insisted, giving the passengers in the back a broad grin. 'Look after those pups!' he ordered. 'Bring them back here safe and in one piece!'

They nodded, smiled and waved.

'Amazing!' Helen said again. Everything in the world was brilliant – the yellow crocuses growing at the roadside, the green moss on the stone walls, the clouds being whirled down Strike Fell by the strong wind . . .

Sally drove on down the hill until they came to the Althams' farm. Turning up a rough, winding drive, she pointed out a small lake fed by a fast-running stream which tumbled down a rocky slope. 'That's Silcott Tarn,' she told them. 'It's a nature reserve with all kinds of unusual birds and plants, but it's out of the way, so not many people know about it.'

Helen and Hannah were too busy trying to calm their restless puppies to pay much attention.

'Sit!' Helen told Tess, as the little cream pup tried to slide off her lap and play with Titch.

'Stay!' Hannah said to Toby, who had leaped up to look out of the window.

Meanwhile, Sally had pulled up outside a small bungalow with a large, modern barn across the concrete yard. As she parked the car, a tall, thin, bald man in a grey fleece jacket, jeans and wellingtons came out of the barn.

'Wait here,' Sally ordered, quickly grabbing her bag and going to meet Malcolm Altham.

The worried farmer shook hands and led her into the metal cowshed.

'I spy with my little eye . . .' Ashley began, looking around at the bare yard and the breezy fell beyond. It seemed to be a game he often played while he waited for his busy mother. 'Something beginning with . . . puh.'

'Puh – puh – puh?' Hannah puzzled. 'Puppy?'

Ashley shook his head.

'Paper?' Helen guessed, pointing to the newspaper on the front seat of the car. Then, as the little boy kept on shaking his head, she gave up. 'OK, tell us!'

'Cows!' Ashley declared.

'Cows doesn't begin with a puh!' Hannah laughed, leaning forward to close the driver's door which Sally had left open in her rush. She forgot about Toby on her lap, who slipped sideways and vanished under the front seat.

'Wait! Don't shut the door, you might squash Toby!' Helen warned.

Hannah hesitated, her hand on the door handle.

And the adventurous puppy seized his chance. He sprang out from under the driver's seat, through the gap into the fresh air. A wild wind bowled him over. He picked himself up, raced for the bungalow and vanished down the side.

'Toby, come back!' Hannah climbed over the seat then tumbled out of the door.

'Tell him to stay!' Helen cried. She dumped Tess on Ashley's lap then scrambled after Hannah, slamming the door behind her.

'Stay!' Hannah yelled, feeling her voice whipped away on the wind. She turned to Helen. 'I'll take this side of the house, you look for him down the far side. We'll meet up round the back!'

Helen nodded. She had to fight the wind to stay on her feet as she set off on the search. Gusts battered her and tore at her hair and clothes, but she made it to the corner of the bungalow.

'Can you see him?' Hannah called.

'No. Can you?'

'No.'

From the shelter of the wall, Helen took a deep breath. She told herself not to panic. Surely Toby wouldn't run far. He would hate the wind and run back to the car. Or he would take refuge on the back porch of the house. No way would he scamper off down the open hillside.

'I'll try the garden,' Hannah shouted.

'Shall I go and fetch Sally?' Helen felt that they

needed help, so she didn't wait for Hannah's reply. Looking frantically this way and that, she ran back to Malcolm Altham's barn.

She found Sally kneeling to examine the black-and-white calf that the farmer had called her about. It lay on a bed of straw, moaning softly, while Malcolm Altham hovered in the background.

'I'll have to take her into the surgery,' Sally informed him, standing up and putting away her stethoscope. 'She needs an emergency operation to remove a partial blockage in her windpipe. If I don't do it straight away, she won't survive.'

The tall farmer nodded briskly. 'Do whatever you have to do.'

Helen hesitated. How could she break in to tell them about the disobedient puppy when they were facing a much more serious crisis?

'Ah, Helen!' Sally spotted her and saw from her face that something was wrong. 'What is it?'

'It's Toby,' she confessed, thinking ahead about what they should do now. 'He's run away again. Can Hannah and I stay here while you two drive the calf to the surgery? That'll give us chance to find him without holding you up.'

Quickly Sally nodded. 'I don't suppose we can leave him to wander about on a strange hillside. But I want you to promise me that you'll look after yourselves.'

'We will.'

'OK, well you do your best to find Toby, but don't run any risks. I'll take Ashley and the two other pups with me. And I'll ring your dad to explain what's happened. He'll probably come along to give you a hand – say in about half an hour's time.'

'Great, thanks.' By now, Helen felt she needed to be outside helping Hannah again. So while Sally and Malcolm Altham gently lifted the sick calf and carried her to the Land Rover, she sprinted round the back of the house to find her sister.

Any hope Helen had that Toby would have showed up was dashed by one look at Hannah.

'Where can he have gone?' Hannah gasped, almost in tears, the wind whipping her dark hair back from her face. 'I've looked everywhere – he's not in the garden!'

'What's over that wall?' Helen staggered into the wind to look beyond the bare flower-beds. Finding footholds, she scaled the high wall, steadied herself on the top and saw an endless sea of rough brown heather dipping towards a stretch of dark water surrounded by rocks. 'Oh no – Silcott Tarn!' she gasped.

It took Hannah a few moments to join her and to remind herself of the position of the nature reserve, which Sally Freeman had pointed out on the way up. Sure enough, the small, narrow lake fed by a waterfall and stretching about a hundred metres along a flat valley, was only a stone's throw from where they stood.

Water. Deep water. Cold, deep, black water surrounded by rocks.

Toby running off in a strange place. Getting lost. Going to stare at his own reflection in the spooky lake.

'Nightmare!' Hannah groaned.

Once more, her scared voice was torn away by the wind. And the clouds rolled in, speeding across Doveton Fell, bringing a dull, dreary darkness to the green hills and heading rapidly for the ridge where they stood.

'Come on!' Fear pushed Helen forward. She

jumped down from the wall into the heather, stumbling on towards the tarn.

Hannah followed. 'What if he ran off in the other direction?' she gasped.

'We'd better check the lake first. You know what Toby's like with water!' In any case, if the puppy hadn't made his way to the tarn, then they could relax a little. The deep lake was what they had to worry about – more than the wild moors and steep slopes to either side.

But there was a lot of lake to search, and Toby was a very small dog. When they reached the boggy shore and scanned the bleak area, Hannah and Helen felt more desperate than ever.

'Where do we start?' Helen muttered. Silcott Tarn seemed to be one of the wildest and most unfriendly spots she'd ever seen. Instead of the sparkling clear water of Doveton Lake, the water in the tarn was brownish-black. The shore was strangled with weeds and tall rushes and the twins' feet squelched in the marshy ground surrounding it.

Grimly ignoring the rapid beating of her heart, Hannah made a plan. 'Let's split up again. You take this near side. I'll make my way across that wooden bridge to the far side.' She pointed out a rotting bridge that spanned the marsh at the top end of the tarn. 'Yell if you see anything.'

Helen nodded and set off along the shore. She felt mud oozing into her shoes, then sucking at her feet as she lifted them. Close by, a brown speckled duck broke out of the reeds, took off and flew low across the tarn.

Hannah headed off in the other direction, calling Toby's name. By now her heart was pounding hard. Any slight movement in the undergrowth made her start and she went to investigate warily, afraid of what she might find.

But the thick bushes and tall, straight reeds hid only moorhens and ducks. The birds would start up as she approached and flee noisily, blown off course by the wind.

'Toby!' Hannah cried, rapidly losing hope.

She came to the bridge and stepped on to its slimy boards. The surface was soaking wet and covered in moss, some of the planks broken in two. And the black water lapped sluggishly to either side, slapping against the upright posts which had snagged a thick tangle of broken branches, weeds and logs round them.

This was just the sort of spot that would have tempted Toby, Hannah realised. He liked high places that let him look down, especially if there was water around.

'Toby!' she called softly, holding tight to the rickety rail in case the wind caught her and swept her off her feet. Was it possible? Had he managed to run this far, through the heather, across rocks and marshland to this precarious perch?

The answer came as a tiny whimper from below.

At first, Hannah thought she was mistaken. She leaned over the rail and listened again.

This time there was no doubt. She could definitely hear a puppy's high, terrified cry.

'Helen!' Hannah called for her sister.

As Helen splashed and stumbled through the marsh towards the bridge, Hannah climbed on to the slippery rail to peer under the platform. She saw tentacles of green, slimy weeds swirl just under the dark surface, and in the shadows a tangle of twigs and logs jammed against the posts.

As Helen drew near, she had a better view of the log-jam under the bridge. 'Oh no!' she groaned.

111

She looked hard in order to be sure.

Yes – there was Toby, up to his usual trick of diving into water and coming up for air. Only this time there was no Speckle to rescue him. What was more, Silcott Tarn was choked with weeds, cold and treacherous.

And Toby had only a piece of sodden timber to cling to, out of reach and slowly working its way free of the log-jam, about to drift out into the middle of the freezing lake.

Ten

The wind cut through Helen. She felt cold to the core, with a twist of fear curling up from her stomach. 'Wait there!' she yelled at Hannah. 'I'll see if I can reach Toby from the shore!'

Plunging into the lake, she waded up to her knees before a hidden current began to pull her sideways. Instead of heading directly for the bridge, she found herself forced away. Her feet failed to get a grip on the slimy rocks which formed the bed of the lake. She stumbled, overbalanced and landed awkwardly, up to her waist in the brackish water.

Seeing Helen fall, and with Toby's frightened cries in her ears, Hannah clambered over the rail of the bridge, hung on to it with one hand and tried to lower herself level with the tangle of branches where Toby had landed. But the drop down to water level was too far. Though the puppy could see her, she couldn't reach him.

From his waterlogged branch Toby whined and cried. His front paws were hooked over the swaying driftwood, but his back legs were dangling in the water. As the branch tilted under his weight, one end worked its way free from the jam and drifted wide of the bridge, carried on the same current that had thrown Helen off balance. Soon, the whole thing could work itself loose and be swept away.

Toby felt his support rock unsteadily. He yelped and struggled to stay in place, clinging on in spite of a ducking he received as the branch tilted once more.

Hannah prayed for him to hang on. If he let go, the current would drag him under, he would be snared in the tangle of underwater debris and might never reappear.

'Toby, stay!' she yelled. If only he'd learned to understand the command they'd tried to teach him in training, then maybe his life could be saved.

'Stay!' Helen echoed. She waded out of the tarn and raced clumsily through the reeds towards the bridge.

Once more the current tugged at the puppy's branch and dragged it under. Again, he was lucky to bob back to the surface, still clinging on hard. His black-and-white head was like a tiny seal's – hair plastered to his skull, blunt black nose just breaking the surface.

'Oh, stay!' Hannah breathed. Her stomach lurched as the driftwood support swung out away from the bridge and broke loose at last.

Helen saw the current seize it and send it sailing out into the middle of the lake. Toby clung on, bobbing and swaying through the weeds.

'Now we'll never reach him!' Hannah wailed, convinced that he would drown.

But Helen made out the direction of the current by watching two ducks bobbing on the water downstream from Toby. It swirled into the centre of the tarn, then swung back towards the near bank, carrying the birds to within three metres of the shore.

The sight gave her fresh hope. If only Toby could hold on long enough . . .

And she needed a branch of her own, or a straight piece of wood. 'Hannah, help me!' she begged, grabbing one of the decaying planks that formed the bridge. Together, they prised the wood free and ran with it towards the bank.

The force of the wind slowed them, but luckily it also held up Toby's progress through the strong current. It meant that Helen and Hannah were in time to meet him as he floated close to the shore.

They found it hard to imagine what the tiny puppy was going through. His eyes must be blinded by muddy water, his whole body stiff with cold. Perhaps he wouldn't be able see them, or perhaps he would lose his grip and plunge into the tarn.

'Stay there!' Hannah urged. She and Helen had waded as far into the lake as they dared, feeling the strong pull of the undertow. Any further, and the water would sweep them off their feet.

Helen lowered the plank on to the surface, held on to one end and floated the whole thing out towards Toby.

'Will it reach!' Hannah closed her eyes for a second, afraid to look.

Toby's branch still drifted towards them, but the puppy's grasp seemed to be slipping. His head sank lower than ever in the water.

'Hang on!' Helen pleaded. 'That's right, Toby; *stay!*'

He seemed to hear above the rush of frothing, swirling water that filled his ears. And for once he understood the vital word. He made no move to let go of his branch until it drifted up against Helen's plank.

Now! Hannah whispered to herself as the precise moment for Toby to jump from the branch to the plank arrived.

'Come here!' Helen cried. She made it sound calm and firm as if they were in a training session, though her heart missed a beat.

A flurry of wind raised the surface of the tarn and whipped a heavy white spray in Helen and Hannah's faces. When they could see again, they made out Toby getting ready to let go of his branch.

'Here, boy!' Hannah cried.

Obeying the command, he plunged sideways from

the driftwood and caught hold of the lifeline that Helen held out for him. With a splash and a desperate lunge, he made it on to the plank.

Tears of relief mixed with the wild spray on Hannah and Helen's cheeks as they quickly pulled him to safety.

'My toes will never ever get warm again in my whole life!' Helen declared. She had a duvet wrapped round her shoulders and her feet were snuggled inside two pairs of thick socks and her furry-rabbit slippers.

'S-s-stop m-m-moaning!' Hannah's teeth chattered uncontrollably. 'W-We s-saved T-T-Toby, didn't we?'

They sat on the floor by the fire at Home Farm, recovering from their adventure, with Speckle, Titch, Tess and Toby stretched out on the rug between them. Toby was already warm and dry, while the twins had yet to thaw out.

'At least he looks none the worse for wear,' David Moore grinned. 'A bit different from when I showed up at Silcott Tarn!'

'Yeah, trust you to wait until the worst was over!' Helen teased. 'You arrive just as we pull Toby out of the lake – no need for you even to get your feet wet!'

'That was good timing on my part,' he pointed out. 'Today's not the sort of day to go paddling!'

'Don't even talk about it!' Hannah shivered. 'Anyway, Dad, I was glad to see you, even if Helen wasn't.' He'd arrived in the nick of time to run down the hill with dry jackets and towels, and a blanket to wrap Toby in.

'Creep!' Helen muttered.

'Hope your toes drop off with frostbite!' Hannah hissed back.

Their dad broke up the argument. 'Back to normal, I see; ever-loving sisters!' He hummed a tune as he put more logs on the fire. A heap of red cinders fell through the grate, while fresh flames licked at the new wood. 'Good news from Sally Freeman, by the way.'

'What did she say?' Helen and Hannah said in unison.

David smiled. 'First they argue. Now they work in stereo!'

'Dad!' Helen pleaded for an answer.

'Let's see.' He stood up straight. 'The first thing was that Malcolm Altham's calf survived the operation. Sally removed the blockage from her windpipe and she's back to normal.'

'And?' Hannah guessed there was more. 'What about Leila?'

'Oh yes, Leila. According to Sally, who rang the Steeles a few minutes ago and then rang me, the dog is able to stand and is even taking a drink every now and then. The vet's official verdict is that she will live!'

Hannah sank back against a chair leg and sighed. 'Yes!'

Helen bounced up from her duvet-cloak, grabbed Hannah by both hands, pulled her up and twirled her round.

'Steady!' their dad warned, standing between the prancing girls and the dogs.

But the pups wanted to join in the celebrations. First Titch, then Tess and finally Toby crept between David's legs and began to play. Titch bounded up on to the easy chair, rolled off and attacked Helen's slippers. Tess fell over Hannah's foot and skidded across the polished floor. Toby yapped and wrestled with Hannah's leg.

'What's all the noise about?' Mary asked, whirling into the room with a blast of fresh air and tossing her car keys on to the table.

Her arrival broke up Helen and Hannah's crazy dance.

'Mum!' Helen cried. 'We've got so much to tell you. We visited Leila, then Toby fell in Silcott Tarn. He nearly drowned, but we were brilliant and rescued him with a plank of wood, and now . . .'

'Whoah!' Mary begged. 'What? When? Where? Why?'

Hannah took her by the hand. 'It's true,' she insisted. 'Except the bit about us being brilliant.'

Helen tutted, but then had to admit that Hannah was right.

'If you really want to know . . .' Hannah went on, leaving her mum's side and going to pick Toby up from the rug. He was warm, soft and shiny, a bundle of speckled energy. '. . . it was actually Toby who was brilliant.'

'He was,' Helen added. 'Totally cool!'

Mary stared at the trio – Toby snuggling up to Hannah, Helen linking arms with her beloved twin sister. 'Explain!' she demanded.

'Toby learned how to stay!' Helen told her. 'We've been trying to teach him for ages, and when it really, really mattered, he did it!'

'He stayed on the branch,' Hannah added. 'He's a clever, brilliant puppy!'

'*Woof!*' Speckle's deep bark broke in on the congratulations. He stood up and demanded attention. '*Woof!*' – *A brilliant puppy, just like his dad!*

HOME FARM PUPPIES 2:
Tess Gets Trapped

Jenny Oldfield

Helen and Hannah are thrilled when their very own Speckle becomes a proud dad. But a trio of lively, loveable mongrel pups brings unexpected problems and chaos to the twins' Lakeland home . . .

Tess is the gentlest of the three pups and follows the twins everywhere. But when they visit neighbour, Jack Steele, Tess chases after a dangerous machine and becomes trapped. While Jack fetches tools to release her, the twins are drawn away by a dog fight. And, when they return, Tess has vanished . . .